HAUNTING OF THE GHOST RUNNERS

DINOSAUR COVE

DINOSAUR COVE™

HAUNTING OF THE GHOST RUNNERS

by
REX STONE

illustrated by
MIKE SPOOR

Series created by
Working Partners Ltd

OXFORD
UNIVERSITY PRESS

Special thanks to Jan Burchett and Sara Vogler.

To Oscar and Lucy Webb,
and all the pupils of Edward Feild School.   R.S.

Dedicated to 'Working Partners' with thanks for all the
encouraging comments.   M.S.

OXFORD
UNIVERSITY PRESS

Great Clarendon Street, Oxford OX2 6DP
Oxford University Press is a department of the University of Oxford.
It furthers the University's objective of excellence in research, scholarship,
and education by publishing worldwide in

Oxford   New York

Auckland Cape Town Dar es Salaam Hong Kong Karachi
Kuala Lumpur Madrid Melbourne Mexico City Nairobi
New Delhi Shanghai Taipei Toronto

With offices in

Argentina Austria Brazil Chile Czech Republic France Greece
Guatemala Hungary Italy Japan Poland Portugal Singapore
South Korea Switzerland Thailand Turkey Ukraine Vietnam

Oxford is a registered trade mark of Oxford University Press
in the UK and in certain other countries

British Library Cataloguing in Publication Data

Data available
ISBN: 978-0-19-272979-8

1 3 5 7 9 10 8 6 4 2

Printed in Great Britain
Paper used in the production of this book is a natural,
recyclable product made from wood grown in sustainable forests
The manufacturing process conforms to the environmental
regulations of the country of origin

FACT FILE

➡ JAMIE'S DAD'S MUSEUM ON THE BOTTOM FLOOR OF THE LIGHTHOUSE IN DINOSAUR COVE IS THE SECOND BEST PLACE IN THE WORLD TO BE. THE FIRST IS DINO WORLD, OF COURSE, THE SECRET THAT JAMIE AND HIS BEST FRIEND TOM HAVE DISCOVERED IN THE BACK OF A DEEP, DARK CAVE. THE BOYS HAVE NEVER BEEN TO DINO WORLD AT NIGHT. IT'S SCARY ENOUGH WITH ALL THE DINOSAURS. BUT WHAT IF DINO WORLD IS . . . HAUNTED?

JAMIE

- **FULL NAME:** JAMIE MORGAN
- **AGE:** 8 YEARS
- **SIZE:** 1 JATOM*
- **TOP SPEED:** 10 KPH
- **LIKES:** FOSSIL HUNTING AND LEARNING ABOUT DINOSAURS
- **DISLIKES:** BEING STUCK INDOORS

Jamie's eye

Jamie's foot

Jamie's hand

*NOTE: A JATOM IS THE SIZE OF JAMIE OR TOM: 125 CM TALL AND 27 KG IN WEIGHT

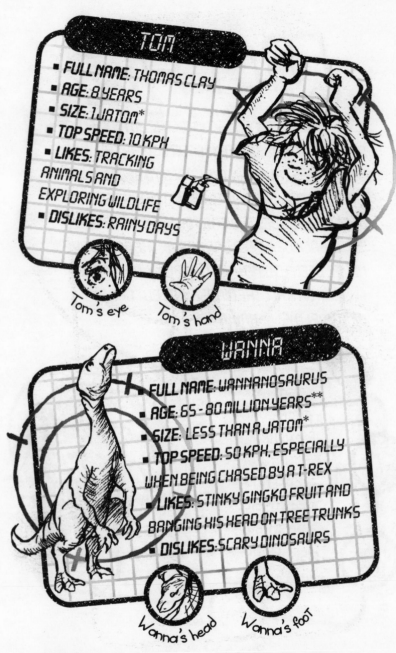

TOM

- **FULL NAME:** THOMAS CLAY
- **AGE:** 8 YEARS
- **SIZE:** 1 JATOM*
- **TOP SPEED:** 10 KPH
- **LIKES:** TRACKING ANIMALS AND EXPLORING WILDLIFE
- **DISLIKES:** RAINY DAYS

Tom's eye

Tom's hand

WANNA

- **FULL NAME:** WANNANOSAURUS
- **AGE:** 65 - 80 MILLION YEARS**
- **SIZE:** LESS THAN A JATOM*
- **TOP SPEED:** 50 KPH, ESPECIALLY WHEN BEING CHASED BY A T-REX
- **LIKES:** STINKY GINGKO FRUIT AND BANGING HIS HEAD ON TREE TRUNKS
- **DISLIKES:** SCARY DINOSAURS

Wanna's head

Wanna's foot

*NOTE: A JATOM IS THE SIZE OF JAMIE OR TOM: 125 CM TALL AND 27 KG IN WEIGHT
**NOTE: SCIENTISTS CALL THIS PERIOD THE LATE CRETACEOUS

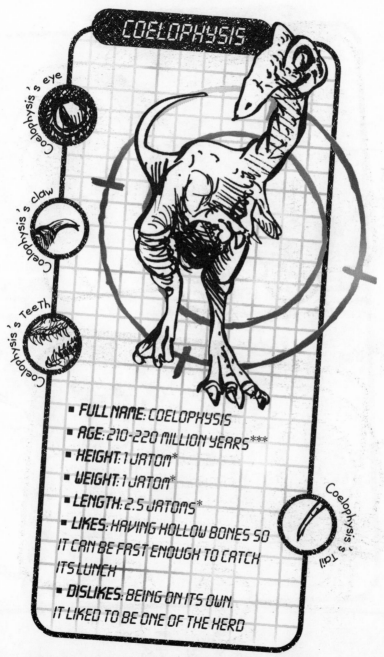

COELOPHYSIS

Coelophysis's eye

Coelophysis's claw

Coelophysis's Teeth

Coelophysis's Tail

- **FULL NAME:** COELOPHYSIS
- **AGE:** 210-220 MILLION YEARS***
- **HEIGHT:** 1 JATOM*
- **WEIGHT:** 1 JATOM*
- **LENGTH:** 2.5 JATOMS*
- **LIKES:** HAVING HOLLOW BONES SO IT CAN BE FAST ENOUGH TO CATCH ITS LUNCH
- **DISLIKES:** BEING ON ITS OWN. IT LIKED TO BE ONE OF THE HERD

*NOTE: A JATOM IS THE SIZE OF JAMIE OR TOM: 125 CM TALL AND 27 KG IN WEIGHT
***NOTE: SCIENTISTS CALL THIS PERIOD THE TRIASSIC

Landslips where clay and fossils are

DINO CAVE

High Tide beach line

Low Tide beach line

Sea

Smuggler's Point

Jamie Morgan cast his fishing line into the black water of Dinosaur Cove. His float landed with a faint splash and bobbed on the gentle waves, its red nightlight glowing in the dark.

'I love fishing at night, but the fish don't seem to like it much,' he said to his best friend Tom Clay, who was sitting beside him on the rocks of Smugglers Point. 'We've got really juicy worms for bait, but we haven't even caught a tiddler.'

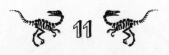

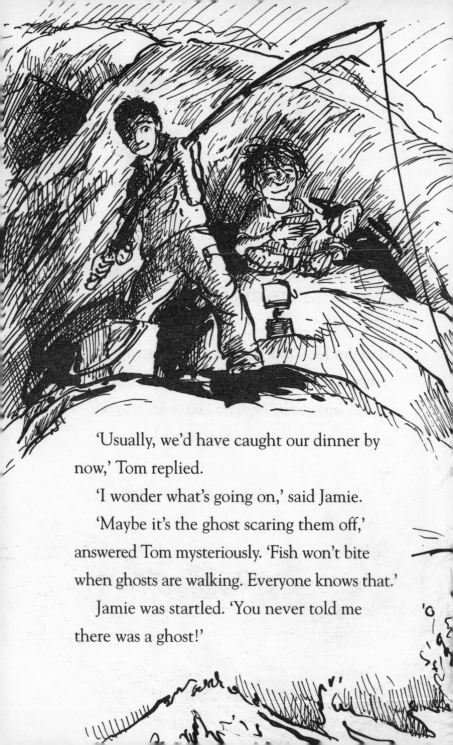

'Usually, we'd have caught our dinner by now,' Tom replied.

'I wonder what's going on,' said Jamie.

'Maybe it's the ghost scaring them off,' answered Tom mysteriously. 'Fish won't bite when ghosts are walking. Everyone knows that.'

Jamie was startled. 'You never told me there was a ghost!'

Unlike Tom, Jamie hadn't lived in Dinosaur Cove all his life. When he and his dad had come to make their home with Grandad in the lighthouse on the cliffs, the boys had become best friends, and Tom always knew all the best places to go exploring.

'Didn't you know?' Tom asked in a hoarse whisper. 'The cove's haunted by a terrifying smuggler from the olden days. Mad Jim McGrew was the most feared man for miles around. He used to land his boat right here and haul his barrels of rum up the sand to hide them from the law. Anyone who tried to stop him disappeared. And on dark, moonless nights like this, his ghost walks again! Even the fish can feel his evil presence.'

Jamie stared at him, open-mouthed.

Tom grinned then shouted, 'Boo!'

Jamie jumped, then punched his friend on the arm. 'Good one!' Jamie smiled. 'I nearly believed you for a minute.'

Suddenly a look of horror came over Tom's face. He pointed a wobbly finger over his friend's shoulder.

Jamie whipped round. A hunched figure was slowly moving across the beach. It was dragging something heavy—something that looked like a barrel.

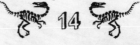

'It's Mad Jim McGrew!' croaked Jamie.
'The story must be true after all.'

At that moment, the lighthouse beam
swept across Dinosaur Cove and the boys could
see an elderly man in a scruffy jumper and
waders pulling a big wicker basket behind him.

'That's not a ghost,' said Jamie in relief.
'It's Grandad!'

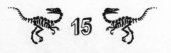

15

Jamie's grandfather stopped and gave them a cheery wave. 'You two look like gawping codfish!' he laughed. 'What's the matter?'

'Tom's been telling me a scary story,' said Jamie.

'We thought you were a ghost,' added Tom.

Grandad chuckled. 'I'm just rescuing one of my lobster pots. It must have broken loose from its moorings and got washed in at high tide.' He pointed to their bucket perched on the rock. 'Caught anything yet?'

The boys shook their heads.

'Fishing's all about patience, lads,' said Grandad, swinging the pot on to his shoulder. 'I'm taking this up to my shed for mending. I'll come back for you later.'

He made for the stone steps that led to the lighthouse.

'Grandad won't be back for ages,' said Jamie. 'Once he gets pottering in his shed he forgets all about time.' He looked at Tom, eyes twinkling. 'I know somewhere really scary, and it's not just a story.'

'Do you mean . . . ?' Tom glanced up at the cliffs behind him.

Jamie nodded. 'Dino World. It'll be super spooky at night.'

'Awesome!' Tom jumped to his feet.

17

'I've got everything in my backpack.' Jamie got up, too. 'Fossil Finder, Triassic ammonite, and we can take our lantern.'

Jamie and Tom had a wonderful secret. They'd discovered the entrance to a fantastic world of living dinosaurs and explored it whenever they could.

'What are we waiting for?' exclaimed Tom. They pulled in their fishing lines and packed up their kit into Jamie's backpack. 'We can leave our bucket and rods in the cave.'

The boys climbed the steep cliff towards the smugglers' cave and the secret entrance to Dino World. It was hard to find their way in the dark without slipping on the loose stones of the rock face but at last they reached the black, gaping hole of the cave.

Once inside they put down their rods and bucket and Tom held up the lantern.

Strange shadows danced over the rock walls as they made their way to the back.

'There are the fossilized footprints,' whispered Jamie. His voice echoed eerily as he placed his feet in the prints and began to follow the trail. He felt the usual fizz of excitement in his tummy—and a little tingle of fear.

'It's going to be really creepy going into Dino World at night,' he said, hesitating.

'Not for bold Triassic explorers like us.' Tom nudged his friend forwards. 'It'll be great!'

The boys started to count as the footprints led them towards the solid rock at the back of the cave.

One … two … three … four … five …

FLASH!

 19

A second later, they were standing in the
familiar hollow tree trunk, staring out at the
dark forest beyond.

Jamie and Tom stepped out on to the crunchy
pine needles that covered the forest floor. The
sparse conifer trees made black shapes against
the deep purple sky. Far away lay the vast desert
and beyond it a line of volcanoes rose up looking

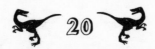

as if they were giant camels' humps in the pale
light from the crescent moon.

The ferny branches of the cycad trees hung
over them like huge spiders and a wispy mist
billowed around their feet. In the distance,
cries and deep rumbling roars filled the night.

'You were right,' whispered Tom eagerly.
'This is extra creepy.'

CHAPTER 2

Animal and insect noises broke the dark silence.

'Dino World's always noisy,' whispered Jamie. 'But it sounds a lot more scary in the dark.'

CRASH!

'Something's coming!' hissed Tom.

They could hear snapping branches and thudding footsteps. Jamie felt his heart beating faster. What was it? Tom held the lantern up but too late! Something small and fast knocked them off their feet.

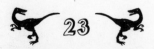

A domed head loomed
over Jamie and he felt hot
breath on his face. All at once
a rough tongue began to lick his hands.

Grunk!

It was Wanna, the friendly little
wannanosaurus who was part of the
Dino World magic and always joined
them on their prehistoric adventures.

'Hello, Wanna!' exclaimed Jamie, trying
to push the excited dinosaur off his chest.

Wanna ran round in circles, grunking
happily.

'I know what you want,' said Tom,
reaching up to an overhanging branch and
picking a handful of orange gingko fruit. 'Your
favourite smelly snack.'

Wanna butted Tom in the back.

'Hey, I'm not a gingko tree!' laughed Tom,
throwing him a treat.

As Wanna gobbled up the gooey fruit, Jamie said, 'I hope you're ready to be our night-time guide, Wanna. We want to go exploring in the dark.'

Kuroak! Kuroak!

'Did you hear that?' said Jamie, taking the lantern and peering into the darkness in the direction the strange sound was coming from. 'Wonder what it is?'

'Let's go and find out,' declared Tom. 'Forward, Triassic adventurers!' He set off between the ferns.

'Hang on!' called Jamie urgently. 'I've forgotten my compass, and without it, we'll never find our way back in the dark.'

'I hadn't
thought of that,' said
Tom. 'We don't want to be stuck
here all night. Pass me the fishing
nightlights. They'll be perfect.'

He turned one on and wedged it into the
hollow tree. It gleamed brightly in the darkness.

'We'll leave one every now and then,'
he explained. 'Then we'll be able to follow
them back.'

'They'll be beacons like the lighthouse,'
said Jamie.

Kuroak! Kuroak!

The lantern lit the way for the three friends
to set off towards the eerie sound. The trees
became thicker and Jamie had to hold up the
lantern to avoid tripping over the dense
ferns that covered the ground. Tom
wedged the fishing nightlights
into the rough tree trunks
as they went.

'The croaking's coming from up ahead,'
said Tom. 'Let's keep go—eugh!' he said as
they walked right through a cobweb.

But Jamie was frozen in one spot, staring
at huge, dark fingers reaching down towards
them from the tree tops. 'Tom?' quavered
Jamie, stepping in front of a frightened
Wanna and lowering the lantern. 'There's
a giant hand coming for us.'

Tom
looked up but
the hand had
disappeared.

'Oops,'
said Jamie,
raising the
lantern again.
'It was just the
shadow of those
hanging branches. Sorry.'

After a few more steps, they had
to hold on to a tree trunk to climb over
some rocks. Jamie reached out blindly for
something to pull himself up on and his
fingers found a smooth surface with two
small pits. He hauled himself up, but then
realized what he'd just felt.

'Is that a . . . a skull?' he gasped in horror.
'Are my fingers in the eye sockets?'

'It's not a skull,' laughed Tom. 'It's a rock with holes—' He broke off as something crawled over his feet.

'Jamie,' he whimpered.

'I felt it too.'

Slowly they looked down. A small turtle, its armoured shell gleaming in the glow of the lantern, had just plodded over their trainers. The boys grinned at each other in relief.

Grunk?

Wanna bent down and gave the turtle a nudge.

The turtle ignored him. It plodded on and disappeared under a spiky frond.

Grunk?

'We're getting spooked by everything!' said Tom with a grin. 'We're meant to be brave Triassic explorers and we're scared of a little turtle.'

'You're right,' replied Jamie. 'Forget being scared. We're going to discover what's making that strange croaking.' He turned to check that Wanna was with them and started in surprise. Something almost glowing was moving between the trees behind them.

'Tom.' His voice sounded very wobbly.

'I thought you said forget being scared,' laughed Tom.

'I did,' whispered Jamie. 'But look!'

Tom turned slowly round. The boys froze as a pale figure flitted away into the darkness and silently disappeared.

Jamie let out a ragged breath.

'Was that a . . . ghost?'

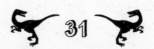

CHAPTER 3

Tom darted forward but the figure had
vanished.

'Now that was definitely scary,' said Jamie
shakily.

'Sure was!' exclaimed Tom. 'Could Dino
World be haunted? That looked really ghostly.'

'I don't know,' Jamie replied. 'But we
probably don't want to find out.'

Kuroak! Kuroak!

'At least *that's* not a ghost!' said Tom. 'Let's
keep going.'

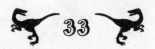

They set off in the direction of the cry, turning nervously now and again to check for signs of their silent pursuer.

Occasionally they caught a flash of something mysterious moving among the trees, keeping its distance.

Tom stopped to put another nightlight into a tree. 'That's the last one,' he said.

'So we can't go any further?' said Jamie, disappointed.

'And we can't go back,' said Tom. 'Not while that ... thing is following. So what do we do?'

Kuroak! Kuroak!

'There it is again,' Jamie said. 'It's really near.'

'And I can hear running water ahead,' Tom replied. 'Let's go and investigate as long as we can still see this nightlight. And hope that whatever ghost is after us doesn't come any closer.'

They stepped into a clearing and saw a shallow stream winding its way across their path, lit by a gleam of moonlight that made the water shine as it trickled on its way. Mist swirled around their feet.

Jamie gasped. 'It's beautiful and eerie all at once!'

Kuroak!

The croaking sound had stopped at the boys' approach but they could see a host of bright glowing eyes. The rocks in the middle of the stream were covered in frogs.

36

'So that's who's making all the noise!'
exclaimed Tom. 'They're like the frogs back
home, except these are sort of bluey-green
and they've got tails.'

 37

'There are tadpoles too,' said Jamie, peering into the water, 'and frogspawn.'

He put down the lantern, eased the Fossil Finder out of his backpack and tapped in the details. The screen on the handheld computer flashed into life.

'*TRIADOBATRACHUS*,' he read. '*TRY-ADD-OH-BAT-RAK-USS. TRIASSIC AMPHIBIAN. UNLIKE MODERN FROGS IT COULDN'T JUMP.*'

The boys kept very still and after a few moments the frogs began to croak again. They puffed out their throats and the skin on their bellies shone red.

'Just right
for a prehistoric
documentary!'
said Tom. He
pretended to hold
a microphone and
whispered to an
imaginary camera.
'At dead of night, deep
in the Triassic forest, our brave explorers
have come upon a colony of frogs. The males
are croaking madly, trying to attract the
females.'

Jamie grinned. He knew his friend's
ambition was to be a TV wildlife reporter.

Churck, churck!

The new sound was coming up from
among the weeds.

'And that's their girlfriends replying,'
laughed Jamie.

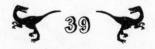

Wanna darted to the
edge of the stream.

Plop! Plop! Plop!

The frogs ran across their stones
and dived into the water. Wanna
plunged his nose in after them.

'And this is astonishing.' Tom kept up the
report. 'A wannanosaurus hotfoot from the
Cretaceous Era has frightened them away!'
He hauled the eager little dinosaur away
from the water. 'Stop it, Wanna.
You're too big to play with them.'

Plop!

'I'll get the
females to come out,'
said Jamie. He sat
down by the stream.
'I'll copy the call of the male.
That should do it. *Kuroak! Kuroak!*'
There were ripples from among the
weeds and a solitary frog scrambled out
of the water and up on to Jamie's lap
with a loud CHURK!

Plop!

Plop!

'Hello there.' He spoke softly to the quivering frog. She was bigger than the males but without the red belly.

Tom laughed. 'You've caught something at last, but you only fooled one of them. The others aren't that daft.'

'Perhaps they're deaf frogs,' joked Jamie. 'Otherwise they'd have all come flocking—my call was so accurate.' He eased the frog on to his hand. He could feel its cold slimy feet in his palm.

'Try not to touch it too much,' Tom reminded him. 'The salt on your hands isn't good for its skin.'

Jamie nodded and carefully held the frog out over the stream. She had just slithered down into the water to join her friends when a twig snapped behind the boys. Wanna gave a warning *Grunk!*

Plip! Plop! The frogs disappeared under water again.

Hearts pounding, Jamie and Tom turned to look behind them. There was nothing to be seen.

'It's our ghostly follower,' whispered Jamie.

'Switch the lantern off,' hissed Tom.

They sat in the dark, holding their breath.

All of a sudden, a pale phantom figure darted between the trees. Then it vanished again.

'I'm not sure I want to find out what that is,' hissed Jamie.

'But we might not have any choice,' Tom whispered back.

'It's just over there!' Tom pointed upstream.
A thin shape was standing stock still on the
bank, the mist swirling round it.

'What is it?' asked Jamie.

Wanna seemed to sense the boys' fear.
He nuzzled between them, trembling.

The mist cleared a little and now they
could see it clearly—a skinny creature nearly
as tall as the boys, with two long back legs.
As they watched it crouched on the bank,
peering intently into the water.

'There's nothing spooky about that,' whispered Tom in excitement. 'It's a dinosaur!'

Jamie flicked open his Fossil Finder. '*LONG, THIN SNOUT,*' he muttered as he tapped in the key words, '*ROWS OF SHARP TEETH, THREE-CLAWED FINGERS* . . . it's a weird name, pronounced See-loh-fi-sis—which means "hollow bones".'

A daring frog popped its head above the water. The coelophysis darted hungrily at it, snapping its jaws and sending up a sparkle of spray as the frog disappeared.

'Oh no!' gasped Tom. 'It's a carnivore. We've led the seely to its dinner!'

A faint rustle in the undergrowth made the boys jump. More seelies were appearing on the bank, like silent ghosts. Their eyes gleamed as they waited eagerly for the frogs to emerge.

'The frogs don't stand a chance,' muttered Tom. 'We have to save them!'

'Got an idea,' Jamie whispered. 'Follow me.'

He made for the broad trunk of a tree growing a little distance from the stream and darted behind it. Tom crept after him, Wanna at his heels.

'I'm going to lure them away from the
frogs,' said Jamie. He cupped his hands to his
mouth and let out a loud *KUROAK!*

'Are you sure about this?' said Tom with a
grin. 'It didn't work very well last time.'

'Wait and see,' replied Jamie, giving
another loud *KUROAK!*

The seelies' heads snapped round.

Thinking it was a game, Wanna joined in
with a few excited grunks.

The seelies heard and drew back, uncertain.

'No, Wanna!' warned Tom. 'We must keep quiet. The frogs are depending on us.'

Jamie tried again and the seelies took a few steps towards the sound.

'It's working,' Jamie whispered.

The band of hungry dinos were moving silently towards them through the ferns, creeping at first, but soon racing eagerly towards Jamie's loud calls.

'They'll be expecting a froggy snack,' said Tom,

taking the pot of lugworms from his friend's backpack and scattering a few on the ground. 'Let's see if this does the trick.'

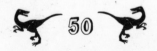

'We'd better retreat though,' warned Jamie. 'We don't want to turn into seely snacks ourselves!'

They slipped quietly away to hide behind the bushy fronds of a low growing cycad.

Just in time! The seelies had already reached the lugworms. They began to sniff them curiously.

'What if they don't like them?' muttered Jamie. 'We haven't got anything else as bait.'

'Not even your grandad's cheese and pickle sandwiches,' Tom replied.

Then suddenly the whole pack was scrabbling for lugworms, snorting and barging each other out of the way. Within a few seconds they'd cleared the lot and were turning back towards the stream—and the frogs!

'Quick.' Jamie put his hands to his mouth and croaked as loudly as he could. This time Tom joined in.

It worked. The seelies began creeping towards them again. Tom tossed some more lugworms down and followed Jamie and Wanna to the safety of a large, ferny bush.

'Great idea of yours,' Jamie whispered to Tom. 'Prehistoric fast food! I think they've forgotten the frogs.'

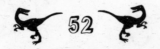

'Let's lure them over here to make sure,' Tom replied. 'It's even further away from the stream.'

They croaked again.

The seelies were suddenly alert. They dashed straight for the boys' hiding place. Tom plunged his hand into the bait pot. But it was empty.

'Uh-oh,' he said. 'We've run out of lugworms!'

'And I don't like the look of those sharp teeth,' cried Jamie.

'Run!' yelled Tom.

The boys and Wanna sprinted off through the trees. The seelies sped silently after them. Jamie jumped over a narrow stream, but as he landed he slipped and fell on the bank.

'It's no good!' Tom panted, pulling him to his feet. 'We can't outrun them. The ground's too uneven. And I bet they've got really good night vision.'

'And a great sense of smell too,' groaned Jamie. He held up his hands. 'Yuck! I'm covered in slimy mud.'

Yuck!

'That's the answer!' exclaimed Tom. 'If we smear mud all over us they won't be able to see us—'

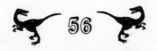

'Or get our scent!' finished Jamie. 'Good thinking.'

The boys scooped up handfuls of mud and slapped it over their arms, legs, and faces and into their hair.

'There are little creatures squirming around in this mud,' said Tom in disgust. 'Eugh! I think I've swallowed one.'

'The seelies are getting close now,' said Jamie in alarm. 'Come on, Wanna. You'd better be camouflaged too.'

As he bent down to Wanna, the little dinosaur jumped at him, taking all the mud off his face in one giant, rasping lick.

'He thinks we're playing again!' exclaimed Tom.

'They've nearly reached us,' warned Jamie. 'Put some more mud on.'

Tom slapped a large handful all over his cheeks and the boys crouched down low, keeping Wanna between them.

The seelies sniffed the air and peered into the darkness, looking just over the boys' heads. After a moment, they turned and disappeared back into the trees.

'Whew.' Tom let out his breath. 'That was close.'

Grunk!

Wanna shook off the mud and climbed out of the stream.

'I think it's time we got back home,' Jamie said, wiping his face.

'Uh oh,' Tom replied. 'I can't see our nightlights anywhere.'

Jamie turned on the muddy lantern and lifted it high, but couldn't make out where they were among the trees.

The boys were completely lost.

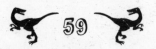

CHAPTER 5

Without the compass and the nightlights to guide them, Jamie didn't know how to get back to the hollow tree.

'What are we going to do?' Jamie asked. 'I don't want to be stuck here all night.'

'Me neither,' Tom said. 'Let's look at the map we've made.'

By the lantern light, Jamie pulled out his notebook and opened to the page with the Triassic map. The boys huddled around it and Wanna poked his nose in, too.

'Look at this.' Tom pointed to the forest area around the hollow tree. 'We never crossed the dried river bed and we're still surrounded by trees.'

'Which means,' Jamie said, catching on, 'that we must be somewhere south of the hollow tree.'

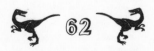

'If we can figure out which way is north, we'll be able to get home!' Tom declared.

They couldn't use shadows because it was night-time, but Jamie remembered that Grandad had shown him how to use the moon to find north.

'I know a way!' Jamie said. 'We're lucky that the moon is crescent-shaped tonight; we can use the two points that the shape makes to figure out north. It's not true north, but should be close enough. Come on!'

Jamie led Tom and Wanna through the forest to a place where they could see the moon clearly.

'All we have to do,' Jamie explained, 'is draw an imaginary line between the two points of the moon, follow it down to the ground and that will point the way south. If we go in the opposite direction, we'll be heading north.'

'Cool,' said Tom, holding up a twig to help see the imaginary line. 'I think it's that way.'

'Me too,' Jamie said.

Grunk!

Wanna seemed to agree.

The three friends set off, hoping they were heading in the right direction. They climbed over some rocks, jumped over a stream and found themselves in a small clearing that they hadn't seen before.

'Did we get it wrong?' Tom wondered.

'I don't think so.' Jamie looked
at the moon again.

Wanna didn't seem to mind. He had
found some leafy cycads with large cones
to munch on at the edge of the clearing.

Thump, thump, thump!

The boys froze. Something was coming
their way. Something big.

'I don't like the sound of that,' Tom said,
as he reached down to turn off the lantern.

'We'd better hide!' Jamie replied, glad that
they were still covered in the mud that would
mask their scent.

Jamie and Tom rushed over to Wanna, who
was too busy gobbling up the cones to notice.
They pulled the little dinosaur behind the dense
cycad leaves just as the branches of the trees on
the opposite end of the clearing began to shake.

A pair of glowing eyes were looking
straight at them!

CHAPTER 6

'Don't make a sound,' Tom whispered, as the creature stepped into the clearing.

Its pig-like head looked small for its enormous body, which had two rows of sharp bumps down the back, but the most frightening sight were the huge tusk-like spikes sticking out either side of its neck.

'What *is* that?' Jamie couldn't risk the noise of taking out his Fossil Finder to look it up.

'I don't know, but it's still coming towards us,' Tom replied.

The armoured creature lumbered into the clearing, sniffing the night air.

Thump, thump, thump!

It paused and then turned away from the boys.

Jamie breathed a sigh of relief but, just then, Wanna lunged towards a cone on the other side of Tom.

'No, Wanna!' Tom hissed, but it was too late. The rustling and the noise made the creature whip its head round to their hiding place.

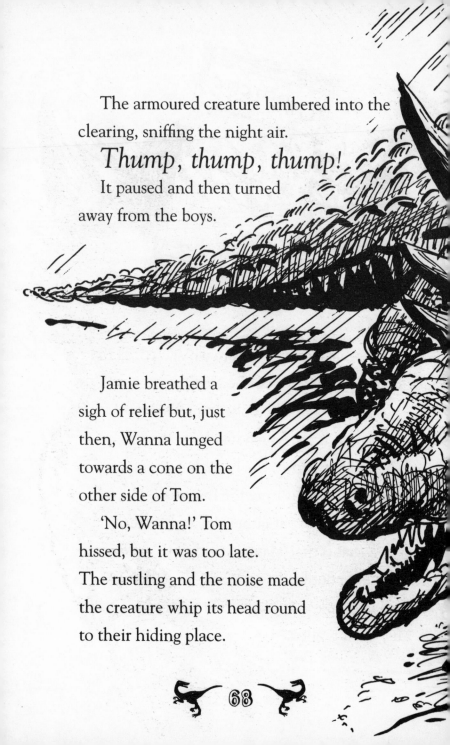

Wanna yanked the cone off the cycad and munched loudly, as the creature came so close, Jamie could feel its breath on his face.

'We're done for!' Tom whispered, closing his eyes.

The creature snorted, opened its mouth and grabbed a cone off the cycad plant, right in front of Jamie.

It chewed even louder than Wanna and Tom burst out laughing.

'It's a herbivore!' Tom said. 'It doesn't want to eat us; it wants the cones!'

As Wanna and the creature had their snacks, Jamie pulled out the Fossil Finder. He typed in '*NECK SPIKES, ARMOURED BODY*' and read out the result. 'It's a desmatosuchus, and those neck spikes could be up to forty-five centimetres long!'

The boys were so close, they could touch the hard armour plates.

'Wow,' Tom breathed as the boys ran their
fingers over the rough surface. 'That's awesome.'

Wanna finished his tasty cone and grunked
happily. He ran about, excitedly, and then
darted out of the clearing.

The boys took one last look at the
desmatosuchus and hurried after him. They
didn't want to lose Wanna in the dark forest.
But Wanna stopped a few
metres into the trees
and wagged his tail.

'What are you doing, Wanna?' Jamie looked around, trying to see what had caught Wanna's eye.

'There's something twinkling over there,' said Tom, pointing through the trees. 'A red light. It's one of our fishing floats.'

'And Wanna found it!' Jamie gave Wanna a big hug. 'Good job, boy!'

'Let's follow the trail,' said Tom, setting off. 'And get back home!'

Soon they were back at the hollow tree, all their floats safe in Jamie's backpack.

Tom gave Wanna a scratch on his bony head. 'See you next time, Wanna,' he said.

The boys stepped

backwards in the footprints until they found
themselves in the smugglers' cave. Picking
up their rods and bucket, they climbed back
down to the beach.

They caught sight of each other in the
lighthouse beam and burst out laughing.
Because anything they brought back from

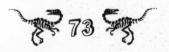

Dino World immediately became millions of years old, all the mud on the boys' bodies had turned to a fine dust.

'If your grandad comes along he'll think we're dust monsters,' said Tom. 'We'll give him a fright.'

The boys quickly washed themselves clean in a rock pool.

'Hello, boys!' came

Grandad's shout,

Hello, boys!

across the beach.
'Have you caught
anything now?'

Jamie grinned at Tom.

'I did catch something,'
he said as Grandad came up.
'But I put it back!'

Grandad would never believe it if
he told him a two-hundred-million-year-old
frog had hopped into his lap.

'Then a whopper came along and nearly
caught us,' Tom told him. 'But it turned out
to be more interested in the plants.'

Jamie's grandad ruffled Tom's hair. 'You
and your stories,' he laughed. 'Let's get home.
There'll be hot chocolate and toasted muffins
for everyone back at the lighthouse. I'll rustle
them up in a jiffy.'

'Awesome!' said Jamie. 'That's the kind of
fast food we like.'

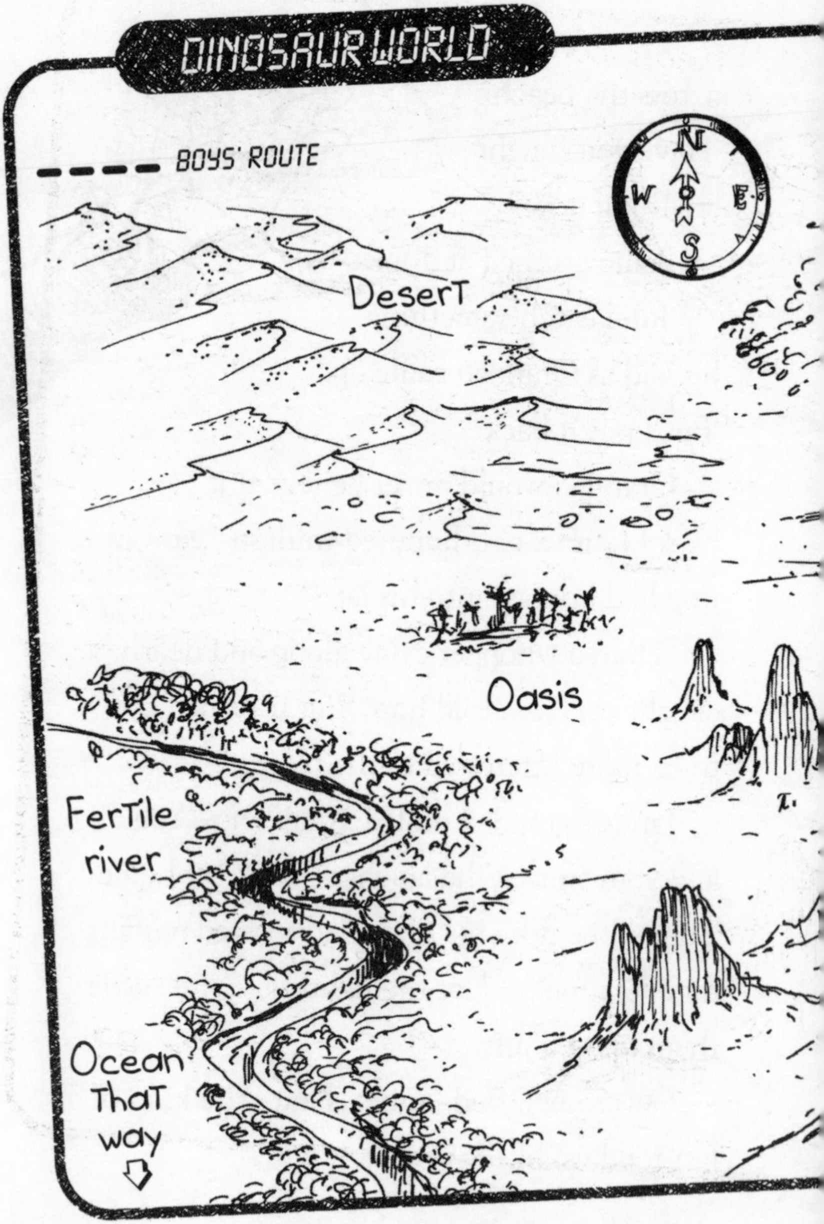

DINOSAUR WORLD

BOYS' ROUTE

N
W E
S

Desert

Oasis

FerTile
river

Ocean
ThaT
way

76

Red Mountain

Forest

Dried out river bed

Hollow Tree

Pond

Scrubland

GLOSSARY

Ammonite (am-on-ite) – an extinct animal with octopus-like legs and often a spiral-shaped shell that lived in the ocean.

Coelophysis (see-loh-fi-sis) – a compact dinosaur that walked on two long legs and was a skilled hunter with large eyes and good eyesight. Its hollow bones helped make it a fast runner.

Cycads (si-kads) – plants with thick trunks, palm-like leaves and cones.

Desmatosuchus (des-mat-oh-soo-kus) – a large herbivore with spiky armour, including two very large spikes at the shoulders, and a shovel-like snout.

Gingko (gink-oh) – a tree native to China called a 'living fossil' because fossils of it have been found dating back millions of years, yet they are still around today. Also known as the stink bomb tree because of its smelly apricot-like fruit.

Triadobatrachus (try-add-oh-bat-rak-us) – a frog-like animal with a small tail. The first fossil was found in Madagascar.

Triassic (try-as-sick) – from about 200 to 250 million years ago, during this time period, seed plants and spiney trees flourished on land along with many species of reptiles and, eventually, the first dinosaurs.

Wannanosaurus (wah-nan-oh-sor-us) – a dinosaur that only ate plants and used its hard, flat skull to defend itself. Named after the place it was discovered: Wannano in China.

You'd better watch out…
we're taking flight